FACE CHALLENGES,

SOLVE PUZZLES,

AND ESCAPE THE BOOK!

The Cursed Temple

Published in French under the title *Journal d'un Noob
– Escape book – Le méga temple maudit*
© 2019 by 404 éditions, an imprint of Édi8, Paris, France
Text © 2019 by Alain T. Puysségur, Illustration © 2019 by Saboten

Minecraft is a Notch Development AB registered trademark. This
book is a work of fiction based on the *Journal d'un Noob* series by
Cube Kid and not an official Minecraft product, nor approved by or
associated with Mojang. The other names, characters, places, and
plots are either imagined by the author or used fictitiously.

Andrews McMeel Publishing
a division of Andrews McMeel Universal
1130 Walnut Street, Kansas City, Missouri 64106

www.andrewsmcmeel.com

20 21 22 23 24 SDB 10 9 8 7 6 5 4 3 2 1

ISBN: 978-1-5248-5886-5 hardback

978-1-5248-5589-5 paperback

Library of Congress Control Number: 2019950719

Made by:
King Yip (Dongguan) Printing & Packing Factory Ltd.
Address and location of manufacturer:
Daning Administrative District, Humen Town
Dongguan Guangdong, China 523930
1st printing—1/13/20

ATTENTION: SCHOOLS AND BUSINESSES
Andrews McMeel books are available at quantity discounts with
bulk purchase for educational, business, or sales promotional use.
For information, please e-mail the Andrews McMeel Publishing
Special Sales Department: specialsales@amuniversal.com.

DIARY OF AN 8-BIT WARRIOR

FACE CHALLENGES,

ESCAPE

SOLVE PUZZLES,

BOOK

AND ESCAPE THE BOOK!

The Cursed Temple

Alain Puysségur

Andrews McMeel
PUBLISHING®

CHARACTERS

RUNT

This is you! You're Runt, a villager!

For a long time, you were THE noob of your village, Villagetown—and probably even one of the worst noobs in the entire continent of Ardenvell. But that was before. Now you are one of the most powerful warriors in the village.

You've proven yourself time and time again, but there is still much to do. The evil, terrible Herobrine still lurks in the shadows of this world. . . .

EEEBS

One day, Eeebs showed up in Villagetown. Eeebs is an unusual cat with the ability to . . . talk. You've always found talking animals a bit weird. . . .

BREEZE

You used to think that Breeze was like everyone else in Villagetown. Then you learned that she'd previously been taken prisoner by Herobrine, whose terrible experiments left her with strange powers. You've developed a strong connection, and you've promised to protect one another no matter what.

HEROBRINE

There are a lot of really horrible things in life: zombies, the noise spiders make when you try to sleep, mushrooms, and, most horrible of all, Herobrine. He is an evil sorcerer. Really evil. He wants to rule all of Minecraftia.

BEWARE, ADVENTURER!

HOW TO READ THIS BOOK

This is no ordinary book. Don't read it from beginning to end, turning from one page to the next. You'll figure out the rules as you go.

Don't go flipping through the book either, because . . . spoiler alert!

Follow the instructions you're given to the letter (or number).

Get a pencil and an eraser. They'll help you on your adventure!

ABOUT THE RESOURCES

At the end of this book, you'll find some game resources. Don't go there first, because you might ruin some surprises. However, there are also hints you can use if you get stuck.

To begin your adventure, go to 01.

01

Today, the mayor of the village summons you. He tells you he has to talk to you about something REALLY important.

"Runt, Villagetown is in serious danger. We need you! Because of your INCREDIBLE strength, intelligence, and charisma, only you can help us."

Well, okay, he might not say that word for word, but that's the general idea.

He then continues, "A week ago, a gigantic temple sprang up from the ocean off the southern coast. Breeze went there four days ago, and nobody has heard from her since. You have to go! Look, it's here."

HHHUUUUURRRRRRRRGGGGG

Your brain may take some time to absorb all that information.

Temple. Breeze. Radio silence. Cookie. Wait, are you sure he mentioned a cookie?

Anyway, if Breeze is in danger, you absolutely have to go! After all, you made a promise . . .

"Very well! I accept this mission, and I will show myself worthy of your trust! We will come back heroes!"

Well, that's what you would have said. Instead, you hurgged slowly.

To take off right away, go to 02. To ask the mayor for more information, go to 14.

02

You hit the road, and since you're such a great warrior, you don't take long to reach the south coast of Ardenvell safely.

Buuuuuutttt . . . it's SUPER HOT out.

You try to pour a bucket of water over your head just to cool off. That might not be a good idea. Your horse almost runs away. . . .

You are now in front of the infamous temple.

Even though you're one of the bravest warriors of the village, you've got to admit that this is pretty scary.

There is a horse tied to a post near the entrance. You're sure it's Breeze's. Did she go in there on her own? Her courage still impresses you. . . .

Aside from that, the place is completely deserted.

Oh no! There is a sign saying:

RUN, POOR FOOLS!

It's signed by the flame of the eternal lantern.
You draw your two swords, just in case.
Just at that moment, a noise makes you jump.

MIAAAOOOW

It's Eeebs, that weird cat. You give him a questioning look.

"You must be wondering what I'm doing here," he says. "I thought you might need some help."

You look at him with curiosity, then nod with the gravity of a warrior.

If you want to go look at Breeze's horse, go to 11. To approach the daunting entrance to the temple, go to 05.

03

Sadly, you have succumbed to the cursed temple.

You have to start your adventure again. Erase all the items from your inventory.

Start again by going to 10. Good luck!

04

You press the right and middle buttons, but nothing happens.

You must have missed something. . . .

Better go back to 44 to read the instructions on the sign again.

05

You slowly approach the temple entrance.

You can't understand how such a big building could have come out of the ocean. Considering the state it's in, it must be really old.

Why did Breeze come here on her own? If only she'd asked for your help . . .

When you are a few blocks away from the huge door, you hear a noise.

CLICK!

It's not a nice kind of "click," the kind that makes you think of completing a task. No. It's more of a threatening "click." Not cool. Like the sound of a trap . . .

You can't move at all.

You notice that you've lost your entire inventory. Well, not quite—you find that you have a strange map. You can check it out at the end of the book in A4 or on the inside covers, if you like.

After a pensive meow, Eeebs says,

"I know that kind of map. Look: there are numbers on it. Those are the places you can go. But you can only move from one place to another by following the lines that connect them. Be careful! Some places are connected by a dotted line. That means you can't go there directly and you'll have to find out how to unlock access—"

"Hahahahaha!" a terrible laugh interrupts the cat. You'd recognize that laugh anywhere: Herobrine. By some strange magic, his huge bright-eyed face appears, floating above your head. "You have fallen into my trap, adventurer! The warriors of Minecraftia clearly aren't very smart. It's almost too easy. Just like the blue-haired girl I locked up in the dungeon, you will never see the light of day again!"

He's talking about Breeze! A knot forms in your stomach. You hope she's okay.

"I'm going to teleport you inside the cursed temple," Herobrine continues. "No one but me has ever managed to exit! Rest in peace, little warrior!"

Herobrine's evil laugh fades as his magic teleports you within. . . .

Check your map and go to 10 to begin your adventure in the cursed temple!

06

You press the left and middle buttons. Nothing happens.

"I think there's something you didn't understand. . . ."

You better go back to 44 and read the instructions on the sign again.

07

You look at the desk a little more closely.

It's emitting a powerful force.

You suspect that it's magic. You remember a similar feeling when you were in the presence of Notch and Herobrine.

You manage to decipher some symbols on the stand. They appear to be from a very old language. The symbols seem to allude to the temple and the power cube. There is mention of a key. . . . Is the cube the key to getting out of here?

You're not sure why, but you have the feeling that someone is watching you. . . .

There's nothing else you can do here. To return to the secret archives to look around some more, go to 35. If you want to go to another room, take a look at your map.

08

You push the button on the far left and the one on the far right of the three-button device.

CRACK!

Congratulations! The wooden panel breaks, revealing a small hole in the stone.

You discover a small iron key.

You add it to your inventory. To do that, go check the box next to it in the list of objects, at the back of the book, by going to A3.

"This small iron key will surely get us out of this first room!"

To use it, you have to combine it with something. To see what you can combine it with, go to A2 at the back of the book to look at the table of combinations. Just go to the line

with "small iron key" to see what you can pair it with. You will see a number that will tell you where to go in the book!

Go to A2 to see what combinations you can make!

09

You take a closer look at the mural in the six-pillar hall, especially at the horde of zombies, and you notice a hidden button!

"Well done, Runt!"

AHA! A noob would have gotten stuck there for sure, but NOT YOU!

You push it, and a hidden passageway two blocks high appears as if by magic, just under the mural.

BINGO!

(You don't really know what this word means. You've just heard humans say that after they've done something they think is cool.)

You've just unlocked access to another room. You do not know what it is, but you can go find out by going to 25. You can also continue to explore the hall by going to 13. Or you can go to another room.

10

The room you're in is not very big. It's impossible to destroy any of the blocks. You can see a small frame. There is also an iron door.

GGEEEEEEUUUUURRRRRHHHHHH

This noise comes from somewhere under your feet, and it's ridiculously scary.

SO RIDICULOUSLY SCARY.

Behind you, you notice a device with three buttons with a wooden sign above them. Go to 44 to take a closer look. If you want to check out the iron door, go to 50. To go look at the small frame, go to 38.

11

You recognize Breeze's horse immediately.

It's tied to a post in the sand and has a bag attached to its saddle. You look inside and find a hastily scribbled note:

GO TO THE HEART OF THE CURSED TEMPLE
OR YOUR FRIENDS WILL DISAPPEAR. . . .
—H

This isn't Breeze's handwriting. . . . Could it be Herobrine's? This has to be the note that led her here.

You look at the temple again. It gives you the creeps, but your concern for Breeze makes you go toward the huge front door. Go to 05.

12

You try to use the small iron key on the device with three buttons, but it doesn't do anything. Eeebs gives you a half-curious, half-amused look.

You should try another combination. . . .

13

You find yourself in the six-pillar hall. It feels like being in the hall of a huge castle.

GGEEEEEEUUUUURRRRRHHHHHHH

That noise again? It sounds like some sort of scream. . . . Just what is going on in this temple? As long as Breeze is okay . . . You have to keep going and find her!

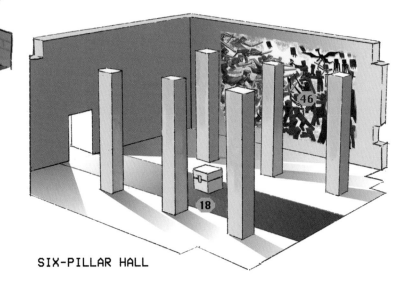

SIX-PILLAR HALL

To go look at the huge mural on one side of the room, go to 46. To open the chest in the center of the room, go to 18.

14

You ask the mayor about the temple. He gives you an apologetic look.

"Sorry, Runt. I've told you everything I know. . . . To be honest with you, I'm worried. Before leaving for the temple, Breeze was really stressed. I think I even heard her mention Herobrine. Above all, you must be careful."

Indeed, if Herobrine is part of all this, you'll have to be very careful. . . .

You decide to set out for the temple. Go to 02.

15

As you slide the feathers into the flask, some bubbles appear. Well done! You have succeeded in figuring out the recipe! You end up with a strange potion. Make a note of it in your inventory!

To continue exploring the alchemy lab, go to 104. You can also keep exploring other parts of the temple.

16

Equipped with the diamond sword, it doesn't take you long to defeat the zombie.

It disappears in a cloud of dust, leaving nothing behind.

You then enter the room it was guarding. The smell of rotting zombie flesh is overpowering. It's horrible.

You discover a small chest that contains a bucket of water. Remember to make a note of it in your inventory!

To return to the secret archives, go to 35.

17

You put the power cube on the device, making sure its icy side touches the ice square of the device.

It suddenly begins to shine intensely.

Part of the room's floor starts moving, thanks to some complicated mechanism involving pistons, revealing a staircase that sinks far into the ground.

You unlocked access to the second level of the cursed temple.

To go to the second level, go to 55. Or you can continue to explore the first level.

18

You can't say exactly why, but something about this chest is reassuring.

Maybe it's because you hope to find some gear in it?

CREEEEEAAAAAAAAK

It opens with a plaintive groan that echoes throughout the hall.

You can't hide your disappointment. You find only a book and a flint and steel.

Don't forget to check them off in your inventory.

You can continue to explore the hall by going to 13, or you can go to a room connected to the hall.

19

The desk in the center of the room is very intriguing.

It's also very dusty. At first glance, it seems not to have been used in a long time.

But you notice a shape on the polished wood.

"Look! It seems like someone recently put something rectangular on this strange desk. You'd better go take a look at the possible combinations; I'm sure you have something you could combine with this desk!"

If you don't have anything you can combine with the desk, you can continue exploring the secret archives by going to 35. Or you can go somewhere else.

20

You open the door.

For a second, there is no sound.

Then a zombie is suddenly upon you!

He is staring at you greedily with his empty eye sockets.

Quick! You have to defend yourself!

Do you have a weapon or something that could help you? If so, don't forget to take a look at the possible combinations. . . .

If you don't have anything you could use to defend yourself, go to 34.

21

With determination in your step, you walk across the study toward the piece of cloth on the floor.

It doesn't take you long to recognize that it's part of Breeze's cloak. By Notch! Your throat feels tight.

Eeebs gives you a sympathetic look. Then he tries to reassure you.

"Don't worry. I'm sure that Herobrine didn't hurt her. Let's hurry up and find her so we can get the Nether out of here. Look: there's a note in one of the folds!"

IN THE HEART OF THE TEMPLE,
YOU WILL NEED THE POWER CUBE.

"It's Breeze's writing. . . ." You let out a sigh. "It seems like she's trying to help me find her. Cross your paws! Let's hope she's okay!"

In one of the folds, you also discover blue orchids. Make a note of them in your inventory!

To keep looking around the study, go to 30. Or you can explore somewhere else.

22

Warning! Do not keep reading unless you've figured out how to unlock access to this area! If you haven't, go back to where you were before.

You take the narrow hallway that leads you to the new room.

Compared to the rooms you've seen so far, it's really small. There's only a torch on the floor.

Although all the blocks in the temple are indestructible, you decide to try to grab it anyway. To your surprise, it goes into your inventory!

Happy with your new find—even though you don't know what you'll use it for—you return to the study by going to 30.

23

You put the small iron key in the small frame. After several seconds, nothing happens.

Eeebs coughs quietly.

> "I don't think that's going to do anything. You should retrieve the key!"

You better go back to 08 to try something else....

24

You attack the wall hanging with your sword, but nothing happens. It seems indestructible. You still feel a draft coming

from behind the fabric. You should go back to 39 to make sure you didn't miss anything. . . .

25

Warning! Do not keep reading unless you've figured out how to unlock access to this area! If you haven't, go back to where you were before.

The new room is very bright. There aren't any torches, but redstone lamps dot the ceiling. In the center of the room, you discover a strange device.

In all your life as a villager—and as a powerful warrior—you've never seen anything like it. It's a very sophisticated apparatus with three squares on top of a quartz block. The one in the center is made of ice.

You look at the temple map and discover that you don't really know where this room leads. . . .

"Let's hope this room takes us to the second level!"

You look at the imposing quartz block a little more closely.

On a small panel on the floor, you read the following:

```
IN THE CENTER, PLACE THE CUBE
SO ICE ABOVE MEETS ICE BELOW.
THEN STEP BACK TO VIEW THE TOP,
AND YOU WILL KNOW THE WAY TO GO.
```

Eeebs asks, looking very serious,

"Well, that's a puzzle worthy of a SUPER MEGA WARRIOR. To solve it, it seems that you need a specific cube. Do we have it?"

If you don't have a cube, you better go to 13 and continue exploring the hall. You can also try to force the device by going to 29.

26

You put the book in the center of the desk, which sends fine particles of dust into the air.

The book opens itself. From the shelves of the library, symbols start flying around the room and into the open book. CRAZY! This reminds you of the effect of a crafting table. In front of you, a passage has appeared.

```
TO GET TO THE SECOND LEVEL,
SPEAK THE MAGIC WORDS AND
THE PASSAGEWAY WILL OPEN.
```

Then there are several sentences in a very old language.

This should help you move forward! Each symbol corresponds to a letter. Look at the first line. The first symbol is the letter I. It seems like you know what some of the symbols mean! Try to decrypt the message! Be methodical and start by inserting all the letters you already know . . .

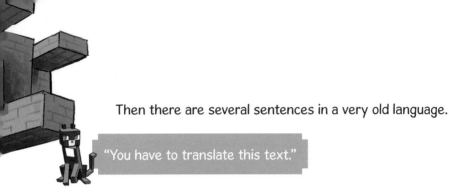

To return to explore the secret archives, go to 35. Or you can go somewhere else.

27

You head for the wooden door of the secret archives. You hear a sound behind it.

That muffled sound reminds you of something, but you can't quite remember what.

There is a sign above the door.

Who could have put this sign here? Weird . . .

You notice that Eeebs's fur is standing on end.

Do you still want to open the door? To open it, go to 20. To continue to explore the secret archives, go to 35. Or you can go somewhere else.

28

You turn to Eeebs, who looks at you even more insistently.

"What?" you ask him.

Holy pixel! You'll never get used to the idea of speaking with a cat.

"I wonder where Herobrine has locked us up. This place looks really old . . . and full of magic."

The same question has haunted you since you set foot in this temple.

Before you have time to say anything, Eeebs adds,

"If you ask me, this place must have been built by sorcerers very, very long ago. Getting out of here is not going to be easy! We have to be extremely careful."

Sorcerers? If he's right, that would explain why Herobrine is the only one who's managed to escape. . . .

To keep looking around the study, go to 30. Or you can explore somewhere else.

29

You look at the device skeptically.

After all this time buried under the ocean, it might not even work anymore.

You decide to try to force it, touching everything, pushing anything that gives way, and even punching the square of ice in the center.

Suddenly, you hear a quiet mechanical noise.

"HAHAHA! There's nothing I can't do!"

Just as you say that, the stone block under your feet disappears, and you fall into lava. Next time, you might want to be more patient.

Your adventure ends here. Go to 03.

30

According to the map, you're in the study.

You notice that there are several desks and some bookshelves.

To take a closer look at the wall hanging, go to 39. If you want to pick up the piece of cloth on the floor, go to 21. Eeebs looks at you insistently. If you want to talk to him, go to 28.

31

You use the flint and steel on the wall hanging.

The hanging immediately catches fire and burns up completely in a matter of seconds. Well done!

You watch the last pixels disappear in a puff of smoke.

With the curtain gone, you see a very small passageway leading to a narrow room. You have just unlocked access to the secret room beyond the study.

To go explore the secret room, go to 22. Or you can continue exploring the study or the rest of the level.

32

You put the bucket of water on the desk. Nothing happens.

You should go back to 19 to try something else.

33

Upon closer inspection, you find a way to get the diamond sword. A light bouncing off the blade allows you to see a button that you didn't notice when you were first looking around the library.

AWESOME!

You push it, and the sword is released. It's a good weapon. You find holding it in the palm of your hand very reassuring. You don't know what horrors are waiting for you in the darkness of this temple. . . . Remember to make a note of it in your inventory.

You can continue exploring the secret archives or go somewhere else. To go back to the archives, go to 35.

34

Unfortunately, you have nothing that allows you to fight off the zombie.

He yells and pounds on you, and you quickly lose consciousness.

Your adventure ends here. Go to 03.

35

You arrive in a new room.

It's so cool! But also really weird. It's a huge library with shelves stretching far overhead. On the map, you see that this is the secret archive.

In the center, a carved column seems to support the whole structure. There is an almost oppressive calm to this room.

SECRET
ARCHIVE

Next to the central column, there is a desk. To look at it, go to 19. You see a wooden door on your right. To go check the door out, go to 27. You also notice a shining frame. To look at the frame, go to 40.

36

You try to attack the zombie with your flint and steel.

Unfortunately, he goes into a frenzy before you have the opportunity to do any damage.

He lands several powerful blows.

As you lose consciousness, one of your last thoughts is of Breeze.

Your adventure ends here. Go to 03.

37

You put the power cube on the device, but nothing happens.

You must have made a mistake somewhere.

The text specifies that the icy sides must touch.

Go back to 25 and try something else.

38

You approach the small frame, full of hope.

Unfortunately, it's empty.

It's impossible to describe how disappointed you feel.

You can go back to 10 to try something else.

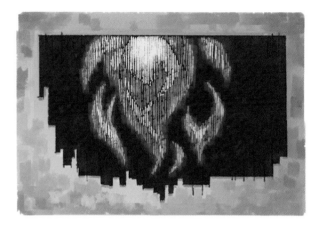

You approach the wall hanging.

There's a huge symbol on it. It looks familiar, but you're not sure. A flame, maybe?

You feel a draft from behind the fabric, but you can't move it or destroy it.

Surely, there must be a way to get rid of it. . . . You should take a look at what you can combine with this wall hanging. Maybe something in your inventory could help you.

If there's nothing you can do here, you can continue to explore the study by going to 30. You can also choose another place to explore.

You take one of the room's narrow staircases to go take a closer look at the shiny object.

The steps creak under your feet and echo throughout this strange library.

In front of you, you discover a display frame. Inside is a magnificent diamond sword.

You want to jump up and down and do a victory dance! This is the kind of sword you'll need to survive in this temple!

Sadly, you can't seem to take it. You try everything, but it remains attached to the frame. Nothing in your inventory seems to interact with it.

You decide to look at it more closely.

There is a quote engraved on the frame.

TO GET THE SWORD, ONLY HALF
THE BLADE IS USEFUL.

JOSHUALD THE GREAT

"The illustrations on the sword's blade are really intriguing, don't you think? Look what Joshuald says!"

If you don't find anything, you can go back and explore the secret archives or go somewhere else. To go back to the archives, go to 35.

41

You raise the book to attack the zombie, and it stops for a second.

If it had eyes, they would probably widen in surprise. It seems like a smile stretches across its face, as though it were unthinkable for you to attack it with such an object.

It hammers you with blows, and, within a few seconds, you lose consciousness. If only you'd had a real weapon to fight it with . . .

Your adventure ends here. Go to 03.

42

With the book in hand, you approach the wall hanging.

You quickly realize that this object will not help you here.

You don't even bother to turn around to look at Eeebs. You know he's probably giving you a strange look.

Maybe you have something else in your inventory that could help you? You better go back to 30 to make sure that you haven't missed a clue. . . .

43

As you get ready to use the flint and steel on the desk, Eeebs gives you an anxious look.

"Are you planning to start a fire here in a library? I must admit I like the idea of keeping all my fur. You might want to try something different. . . ."

Maybe you have something else that you could combine with this desk. Go back to 19 to make sure you haven't missed a clue.

44

You approach the device with three buttons.

"A puzzle! I suspect this isn't the only one we'll encounter in this temple. . . . If we solve it, I bet it will give us a number that will tell us where to go. If you get stuck on a puzzle, you can ask me for advice. To do that, you just have to go to A1, at the back of the book. Okay! Let's take a closer look at these buttons."

You can go back to 10 if you want to try something else.

45

As you utter the phrase you just decrypted out loud, you hear strange magic throughout the secret archives.

The ground shakes a little, and a blinding light comes out from between the pages of the book.

In front of you, above the desk in the secret archives, a mysterious cube has appeared, suspended midair, turning slowly.

It's so strange! You've never seen anything like it. . . .

Maybe it's a trap . . . but you can't resist grabbing the object.

To get the cube, go to A5, then come back here. Don't forget to note it in your inventory.

When you have the cube in your hands, inscriptions and bright symbols appear on the desk.

To look at them more closely, go to 07.

The mural is really huge! You've never seen anything like it. Who could have made that?

It's a painting of a big battle scene, showing the protectors of Minecraftia. How do you know that? Because they look SUPER COOL, and they're totally classy. They're facing an army of terrifying monsters.

"Something about this mural bothers me, but I can't quite put my paw on it. Do you see anything?"

If you don't find anything, you can always go back to 13 and try something else.

47

Sadly, you have succumbed to the cursed temple.

You have to start your adventure again. You can start from the beginning if you think you missed something important.

Erase all the items from your inventory.

Or, to start again just before reaching the second level, go to 55. Then erase all the items in your inventory following the bucket of water on the list.

Good luck with your new adventure!

48

Certain of your choice, you jump onto the first wood block. But you can't see any wood blocks you can jump to next. . . .

You try to start again and jump to a dirt block. Suddenly, all the blocks disappear, and you fall into the darkness.

You hit the ground and lose consciousness.

Your adventure ends here. Go to 47.

49

You slip the small iron key into the lock of the iron door. You hear the latch click.

GREAT! You have unlocked access to the six-pillar hall.

You find yourself in a huge room bathed in light.

To explore it, go to 13. Or you can go to one of the rooms connected to it.

50

You approach the iron door.

You look through its bars and see a much larger room.

Unfortunately, the gate is locked.

You'd better go back to 10 to see whether there is anything else you can do.

51

You look in the furnace and discover a slightly burned piece of paper. You begin to read aloud from the part that hasn't been consumed by the flames.

" . . . that is why a dark terror reigns in the heart of the temple. A terror that no one would ever want to face. The dark, the terrible, the fierce cursed king."

GGGGGEEEEEEEUUURRRRRRHHHH

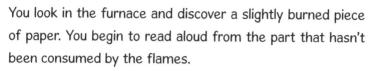

"That's right. There's something I really don't want to meet in this place! We'd better find some gear, in case we bump into it."

You can continue to explore the mineral room by going to 58. Or you can go to another room.

52

You place your hand confidently on the iron block. In front of you, behind the device, a door appears. You have unlocked access to the treasure room!

Your heart is thumping. You are so EXCITED!

If in addition to saving Breeze, you'll be able to return to the village with a treasure, it will be a triumph!

To go explore this new room, go to 86. Or you can continue exploring elsewhere.

53

The closer you get to the throne, the bigger it looks. It's made of diamond, gold, and iron blocks.

Eeebs trots up the first steps and says,

"Look at this! The throne has been vandalized. . . . There are sword marks everywhere. Someone carved 'the throne of the cursed king' into this gold block."

As Eeebs utters these words, a terrifying noise makes the whole temple shake.

GGGGGEEEEEEUUURRRRRRHHHH

"I don't know who's making that noise, but I don't want to meet them. . . . What if it's the cursed king?"

You're scared, but you decide not to listen to Eeebs and continue exploring the old throne room by going to 65. You can also go explore another room.

54

You jump quickly on the first stone block. Unfortunately, you find yourself stuck, and you have no choice but to jump on another kind of block, hoping to get out of it.

Suddenly, all the blocks disappear, and you tumble into the abyss.

You hit the ground and lose consciousness.

Your adventure ends here. Go to 47.

55

Warning! Do not keep reading unless you've figured out how to unlock access to this area! If you haven't, go back to where you were before.

You arrive in the first room of the second level.

"This is the entrance to the second level. . . ."

Well, it's not any more welcoming than the first!

"If you think you've forgotten something on the first level, remember that you can always go back to explore it by starting in this room."

You find yourself in a dark room. On the far side of the room, you can make out a door. But A HUGE PIT separates you from the other side. It's so deep you can't even see the bottom.

In the dim light, you notice a few blocks suspended in the air above the darkness.

To look at those blocks more closely, go to 68. To jump into the void, go to 61. Who knows? Might not be too deep. You can also return to the first level to explore it more as Eeebs suggests.

56

This diamond shield is likely to be very useful in this cursed temple. So you choose to grab it. Make a note of it in your inventory.

While you are putting away the shield, the sound of stone being scraped makes you shiver.

"Runt, look out!"

The golem you took the shield from has started moving and is about to attack you. He's terrifying! You don't have a second to lose! You have to react!

You can go take a look at the combinations you can make in this situation. There might be one that can help.

Otherwise, you can try to escape by going to 81.

57

No sooner have you put your hand on the lapis lazuli block than you are struck by lightning. You chose the wrong block. A sentence comes back to you: "But don't pay attention to those next to the one that lights up when you touch it."

The redstone makes light, and the lapis lazuli block was right next to it. . . . You lose consciousness.

Your adventure ends here. Go to 47.

58

Warning! Do not keep reading unless you've figured out how to unlock access to this area! If you haven't, go back to where you were before.

You are amazed by what you see.

The irregular walls of the room are full of all kinds of mineral blocks. There are some you recognize, and there are some you've heard of or read about, and there are some you know nothing about.

It's MAGNIFICENT! This temple is really incredible. . . .

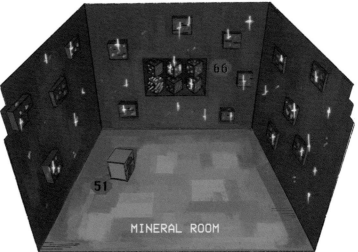

MINERAL ROOM

In one corner of the room, there's a furnace. In a wooden device on the wall are six blocks. To open the furnace, go to 51. To take a look at the device, go to 66.

59

As you put your hand on the emerald block, a pain like nothing you've ever known cements you to the spot. You've chosen the wrong block. You suddenly remember: "The correct block is not green." Of course! The emerald block is green. It couldn't have been the right one. . . . You lose consciousness.

Your adventure ends here. Go to 47.

60

The wall on the left of the room has some strange inscriptions.

TO ACCESS THE ALCHEMY LAB, PROVE THAT YOU ARE WORTHY! COMPLETE THE GRID BELOW, MAKING SURE THAT THE SYMBOLS APPEAR ONLY ONCE IN EACH LINE, IN EACH COLUMN, AND IN EACH SQUARE.

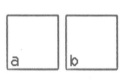

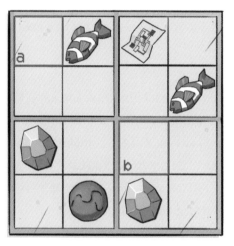

WHEN YOU HAVE COMPLETED THE PUZZLE, MAKE NOTE OF THE SYMBOLS IN "A" AND "B." BELOW, YOU WILL SEE THAT EACH SYMBOL MATCHES A NUMBER. "A" AND "B" WILL TELL YOU WHERE TO GO NEXT.

IF WHERE YOU END UP MAKES NO SENSE,
YOU'VE MADE A MISTAKE SOMEWHERE. . . .

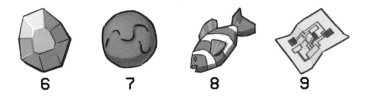

| 6 | 7 | 8 | 9 |

You can continue to explore the old throne room by going to 65. You can also go explore another room.

61

You step back then run and jump into the void. Let's do this! As you plunge into the darkness, the room starts spinning around you. You are completely surrounded by darkness. You can't see anything. You can't hear anything.

After a fall that seems to never end, you hit the ground and lose consciousness.

Your adventure ends here. Go to 47.

62

You put your hand on the gold block, and a powerful electric charge runs through your body. You've chosen the wrong block.

You understand then: "You will have to look next to the gold" means that it's not the gold itself. . . . You lose consciousness.

Your adventure ends here. Go to 47.

63

You approach the brewing stand and notice that there is a potion in progress. How long has it been there? Almost certainly a very long time. . . . It's not finished. All the ingredients have been prepared, and all that remains is to mix them together.

But you still have to figure out the correct amounts of each.

There is a piece of paper that the previous alchemist used, but the recipe looks incomplete.

$$\text{🌑} + \text{🌑} = 20$$
$$\text{🦴} + \text{🌑} = 15$$
$$\text{🪶} + \text{🦴} + \text{🌑} = 30$$

$$\text{🌑} = 10 \quad \text{🦴} = 5 \quad \text{🪶} = ?$$

"Look, Runt! We know how much of the spider's eye and bone to use. We have to figure out how many feathers we need to make the potion. Once we figure out that number, we just have to go to its corresponding section. There is only one possible solution. If where we end up makes no sense, it'll be because you've come up with the wrong answer. If that happens, come back here and try again!"

To continue exploring the alchemy lab, go to 104. You can also keep exploring other parts of the temple you have access to.

64

You attack the warrior golem with your diamond sword. He is not very bright, so it doesn't take you long to land a powerful blow.

The shock bounces up your arm, and you lose your balance. The golem seems practically indestructible.

It takes advantage of your surprise to hit you with its huge fist.

You can't dodge the blow, and you lose consciousness.

Your adventure ends here. Go to 47.

Warning! Do not keep reading unless you've figured out how to unlock access to this area! If you haven't, go back to where you were before.

You step into the old throne room. A strange thrill runs through every pixel of your body. You've already been surprised by a lot of things in this temple, but this . . .

At a glance, you can tell that this place was once radiant. In the center of the room is a magnificent throne.

It's big—HUGE! You wonder who it might have belonged to. . . .

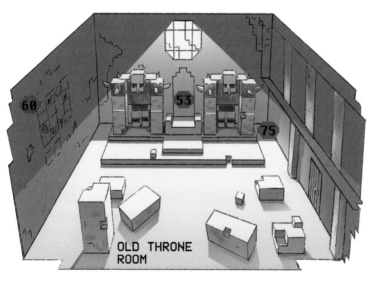

OLD THRONE ROOM

On either side of the throne, there are two statues of warrior golems. You also see strange marks on the left wall. To go look at the statues, go to 75. To check out the marks on the wall, go to 60. To take a closer look at the throne, go to 53.

66

As you approach the strange wooden device with six mineral blocks, Eeebs says,

"I've seen devices like this before. They're very, very, dangerous. . . . You have to choose one of these six blocks and touch it to unlock the passageway to another room. If you're wrong, it's all over for us, so choose well. Look! Here are the instructions."

THE CORRECT BLOCK IS NOT GREEN. IT'S NOT UNDER THE MATERIAL THAT BUCKETS ARE MADE OF. TO FIND IT, YOU WILL HAVE TO LOOK NEXT TO THE GOLD.

BUT DON'T PAY ATTENTION TO THOSE NEXT TO THE ONE THAT LIGHTS UP WHEN YOU TOUCH IT.

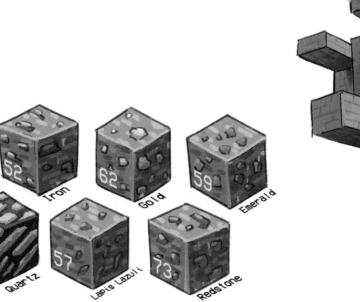

You can continue exploring the mineral room by going to 58. Or you can explore another room.

67

You decide to use the torch you found on the first level to light the room.

It works! Awesome!

You've just unlocked the mineral room, where you couldn't see anything until now. You can look around the room by going to 58.

You can also continue exploring other rooms. When you want to return to the mineral room, you can go directly to 58. If you think you might forget this, write it down somewhere.

68

Throughout the room, there are a lot of different kinds of blocks hovering in the air. They are the only way to cross the room and reach the door on the other side.

You notice a small sign that seems like a warning.

TO REACH THE OTHER SIDE OF THE ROOM, YOU NEED TO JUMP FROM ONE BLOCK TO ANOTHER. WARNING! YOU CAN ONLY JUMP TO THE SAME KIND OF BLOCK AS THE ONE YOU STARTED ON. OTHERWISE, THEY WILL DISAPPEAR!

"This is not going to be easy. . . . It means that if you start on a stone block, you can only jump to other stone blocks."

The sign says that you can jump straight or diagonally but that you can't jump more than two blocks at a time. You look at the map of the blocks.

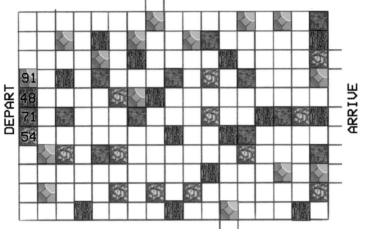

DEPART

91
48
71
54

ARRIVE

Here are the moves you can make from the block you're standing on.

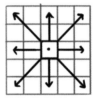

Choose which block you want start on.

When you're done, go to the number of the kind of block you started on.

To go back and try something else, go to 55.

69

Eeebs is a cat! He must be able to see in the dark!

"Eeebs, you're a cat. Surely you can see something!" you say.

Silence.

"Eeebs?"

You hear a sound like a throat clearing.

"Well, actually . . ." he mutters. "Um . . . how do I say this? . . . Despite being a cat and all, I can't see in the dark."

It's your turn to let a heavy silence fall between you. You can't help but think that this cat is a real noob.

You can choose to combine something else with the dark room. Or you can return to the old throne room by going to 65.

70

As you put your hand on the quartz block, all the energy suddenly drains out of you. You understand that you have chosen the wrong block: "It's not under the material that buckets are made of." Iron is used in making buckets, and the quartz was below it. . . . You lose consciousness.

Your adventure ends here. Go to 47.

71

You choose to cross using the dirt blocks. Carefully, you jump on one dirt block after another. While you are doing your last jump, you almost touch a wood block. Your life as a warrior

flashes before your eyes! Fortunately, you come out of it alive, but barely.

You finally arrive on the other side of the room. You can now access a new room, the old throne room. To go to the old throne room, go to 65.

72

You arrive in a new room. When you decided to come here, you read that it was the mineral room. Unfortunately, the room is completely dark. . . . You can't even see the end of your pixels.

"I think you should try a combination."

You can follow his advice or return to the old throne room by going to 65.

73

As you put your hand on the redstone block, you feel like electricity is passing through your entire body. You've got the wrong block! You suddenly understand why. "To find it, you will have to look next to the gold." The redstone block was not next to the gold block. . . . You lose consciousness.

Your adventure ends here. Go to 47.

74

By combining gunpowder with the strange potion, you get a volatile strange potion. Make a note of it in your inventory!

"Great! I think you just have to throw it at this door."

That's what you do. The door then disappears in a bubbling of pixels. You have just unlocked access to a new room.

You read that this is the gallery of heroes. To go there directly, go to 95. Or you can go explore another room.

75

You decide to take a closer look at the two statues. They make you think of stone golems, only fancier.

Eeebs is flabbergasted.

"Check out those statues! My fur is standing on end just looking at them. They're supposed to be warrior golems, and those don't exist anymore. It looks like they're about to move at any second. . . ."

He's not wrong. The statues are really scary. And you've seen a lot of scary stuff, but this . . . On top of that, they look completely indestructible.

One of them is holding a diamond shield. To try to take it, go to 56. To continue exploring the old throne room, return to 65. You can also go explore another room.

76

You have the flint and steel in hand, and you're looking around for something to burn so you can create some light.

Eeebs suddenly stops you.

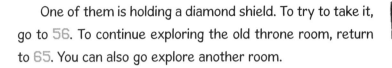

"Are you sure you want to use the flint and steel? I don't know if that's a good idea. . . . What if the room is full of wood? We'd end up roasted in a heartbeat!"

You hate to admit it, but he's not wrong. You put away the flint and steel.

You can choose to combine something else with the dark room, or you can return to the old throne room by going to 65.

77

When you press one of the buttons on the cube, you hear a quiet mechanical noise. Suddenly, you hear another sound. Just as you realize what's happening . . .

BOOM!

You got the wrong button! You are hit by the explosion! You lose consciousness.

Your adventure ends here. Go to 47.

78

You complete the grid with the different symbols.

By some strange magic, the stone blocks disappear one after another.

You've just unlocked access to the alchemy lab.

To go to the alchemy lab, go to 104. You can also continue exploring the old throne room by returning to 65.

79

You hide behind the diamond shield you just stole.

The warrior golem just seems to get angrier. It starts charging and falls on you, uttering deep, guttural cries.

The shield is a poor defense against the creature's fury.

You lose consciousness as the golem clobbers you.

Your adventure ends here. Go to 47.

80

You see many strange symbols and incomprehensible equations in the picture. But there's one sentence you do understand.

> THE POTION YOU CREATE IN THIS
> ROOM WILL BE USEFUL, BUT YOU
> WILL THEN REQUIRE GUNPOWDER.

Strange . . .

You can go back and continue exploring the alchemy lab by going to 104. Or you can go explore another room you have access to.

81

This golem seems far too powerful to you. You'd never be able to beat it. At least not with so little gear. You decide to run away.

After several strides, a smile stretches across your face. You seem to have escaped the creature. But, suddenly, it's in front of you, and you slam right into it. How was it so fast?

Sadly, you will never know the answer to this question, because the golem lands an extremely powerful blow, and you lose consciousness.

Your adventure ends here. Go to 47.

You press one of the buttons on the levitating cube.

For a second that seems never-ending, nothing happens. ABSOLUTELY NOTHING.

Then, very slowly, the cube moves to the wall at the end of the corridor and stops there. It opens suddenly, like a chest, and releases an incredible energy that spreads across the stone blocks of the walls.

After a few seconds, the light fades, revealing a dark passageway surrounded by obsidian.

You have just unlocked access to the dungeon.

"I don't want to be a pessimist," Eeebs says, "but this is the last room in the temple. Breeze has to be here, but I'm worried she won't be alone. . . . I hope you're fully prepared and you've found enough gear. If you haven't, you can always go back and explore the temple and return to the dungeon later."

To continue to the dungeon, go to 98. Or you can keep exploring the temple.

83

You adjust the power cube so it sits correctly on the stone base. Immediately, the wall at the end of the room emits an intense light. You have to shield your eyes.

An armor stand has just appeared with a diamond helmet on it. You decide to take it. Make a note of it in your inventory.

You break the silence. "That's going to be super useful!"

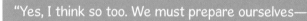

"Yes, I think so too. We must prepare ourselves—"

Eeebs does not have time to finish his sentence.

GGGGGEEEEEEUUUURRRRRHHHH

You share a worried look.

You can continue exploring the temple.

84

You jump to a stone block sticking out from the lava. You continue across the room until you arrive at the other side. There is nothing. There is no opening.

As you get ready to turn around, an ember rises from the lava and sets your clothes on fire. You panic, slip, and join the room's treasure in the lava. You lose consciousness.

Your adventure ends here. Go to 47.

85

Carefully, you combine the strange potion with a blue orchid. It makes a little "Poof!" And then nothing.

The potion didn't become volatile, but you wonder whether it might have other properties. Maybe if you drink it, you could go through the door.

You share your thoughts with Eeebs.

"After all the strange things we've seen . . . But what if the potion has become poisonous? Be very careful."

You can choose to drink the strange potion you added an orchid to by going to 92, or you can return to 99 and try another combination.

86

Warning! Do not keep reading unless you've figured out how to unlock access to this area! If you haven't, go back to where you were before.

You are thrilled that you've unlocked access to the treasure room. Given the size of this temple, you imagine a myriad of emeralds and rare items.

NOTHING.

Well, it's not really nothing, but there's no treasure! The room is full of lava. The decorative glass and stone ceiling that once contained the boiling liquid has collapsed.

You imagine the treasure disappearing with a "sssshhhh" and a thick cloud of smoke.

> "I don't think we can cross this room . . . unless you have water, which would turn the lava into obsidian."

If you have a bucket of water, you can use it by going to 93. Or you can try to jump on the blocks that stick out from the lava and cross the room by going to 84. Otherwise, you can keep exploring the second level from the mineral room by going to 58.

87

There must be another way out of here!

Just like Eeebs, you search everywhere while avoiding the sand blocks falling from the ceiling. You soon understand that you're trapped. Breeze mentioned music. . . . You must have missed something that could have been useful here.

With huge quakes, the whole temple collapses on itself. You lose consciousness.

Your adventure ends here. Go to 47.

The levitating cube in the back of the room seems like a new puzzle.

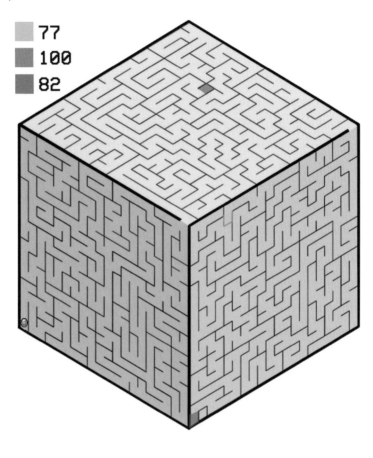

77
100
82

It's absolutely fascinating! Each of its sides is a maze. An emerald is stuck in the middle of it. On one of the sides of the cube, you can see three buttons. You see a sign with instructions.

YOU CAN LEAD THE EMERALD TO ONLY ONE OF THE THREE EXITS. IT'S UP TO YOU TO FIGURE OUT WHICH ONE AND TO PUSH THE RIGHT BUTTON!

THIS WILL LEAD YOU TO THE DUNGEON. BUT BEWARE, CHOOSE WELL, BECAUSE IF YOU MAKE A MISTAKE, YOU WILL REGRET IT.

"Runt! There are three buttons, each associated with one of the exits. . . . You have to try to find the right way to see which of them is the correct one!"

You can also return to the gallery of heroes by going to 95. Or you can explore the rest of the cursed temple.

89

What remains of the cursed king disappears in a cloud of silver particles that scatter throughout the room.

Then the whole temple starts to shake. You think it might fall on you!

You run to Breeze and lift her gently off the ground. She's so weak.

After checking all the cells, Eeebs says,

"Runt! We're trapped! There's no way out! The temple is going to collapse!"

The shaking becomes more and more violent as sand blocks fall everywhere. Then you hear Breeze trying to speak. "Music . . . Runt . . . Only music can get us out." Then she faints.

Breeze's words don't make much sense, but you know you can trust her.

If you have a jukebox, go to 106; otherwise, go to 87.

90

Breeze mentioned music. There must be a reason!

You retrieve the jukebox from your inventory.

As soon as the cursed king sees it, he erupts in anger and screams.

"If you want my opinion, I don't think he likes music," says Eeebs.

As you place the block and put on some music, the king storms toward you, brandishing his sword and shaking the ground with each step. A strange melody fills the dungeon as you run to evade the king's blows, praying to Notch that he doesn't catch you.

"Runt, look! A passage has just appeared! It must be because of the music."

Unfortunately, you stumble on a slab of stone protruding from the floor.

The shadow of the cursed king looms over you. He has caught up to you and has his incredible weapon raised above his head. He brings it down with one strike. You lose consciousness.

Your adventure ends here. Go to 47.

91

You choose the diamond blocks and confidently jump onto the first one.

After a few jumps, you realize that you won't be able to reach the other side of the room.

However, your jumping does lead you to the side of the room, where you discover a passage. To take the passage, go to 103. To go back and choose another kind of block, jump to 68.

92

You decide to drink the strange potion. As soon as you take a sip, everything starts spinning around you.

Suddenly, you remember what you once learned: To make a volatile potion, you need a different ingredient! You made a mistake and have swallowed a powerful poison. You lose consciousness.

Your adventure ends here. Go to 47.

93

You take the bucket of water and start pouring it into the room so that you can clear a path. As crazy and awesome as it sounds, the bucket never seems to run out of water.

When you arrive at the back of the room, you discover there's no door.

As you prepare to turn back, a stone block just above the lava captures your attention. You approach it and discover some strange symbols.

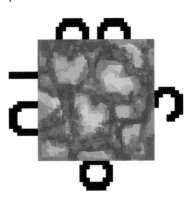

You find instructions near it.

PLACE THE CUBE SO THAT STONE TOUCHES
    STONE. ADJUST THE SIDES AND READ
COUNTERCLOCKWISE, STARTING WITH THE
TOP. YOU WILL THEN KNOW WHERE TO GO.

"The riddles in this temple keep getting harder and harder. Runt! We must be getting closer to our target. Breeze can't be far. Doesn't this riddle remind you of something? You have to put the power cube on it! These symbols on the sides . . . I'm sure there are some on the cube that match up with them! You just have to place the cube in a very specific way."

There is only one possible solution. If where you end up makes no sense, you've made a mistake somewhere.

If you can't find anything, you can also go back and explore the second level. Remember to write down this number, 93, somewhere, so you can come back later.

94

You put the power cube up against the mirror-wall, and the room changes before your eyes. It's as though there was an enchantment that was hiding the dungeon.

The room is dark and menacing. It's full of cells with iron bars and bloody netherrack. There is a horrible, sticky smell.

You advance slowly, all your senses on alert. You see something lying on the ground ahead of you.

"Breeze!" you cry out.

You run to her. She is very weak.

She gives you a reassured look and whispers, "Beware of the cursed king, Runt! Fight only if you are armed. The music . . . don't forget the music. . . ." Then she faints in your arms.

You try to shake her awake when . . .

GGGGGEEEEEEUUURRRRRRHHHH

"Runt, behind you!!! It's the CURSED KING!"

You turn and are suddenly face to face with an abominable creature. It must be TWICE your size, clad in armor weathered by centuries. You can't see its face, just two glowing eyes fixed on you!

If you have the diamond sword and the other two pieces of diamond gear, you can fight the creature. To fight it, go to 97. Breeze just mentioned music. If you have the jukebox, you can try to use it by going to 90. Or you can try to escape, carrying Breeze, by going to 102.

95

Warning! Do not keep reading unless you've figured out how to unlock access to this area! If you haven't, go back to where you were before.

The gallery of heroes is actually a long hallway. It must have been resplendent at one point in time. Several pedestals and murals dot both sides of a carpet that crosses the room. This place was surely built to honor long-lost heroes and warriors.

The gallery is in bad shape. Several pedestals have collapsed, and stone blocks have fallen from the ceiling. At the end of the hallway, you see a cube that seems to be levitating. To take a look at the pedestals and murals, go to 101. To look at the levitating cube, go to 88. You can also go back and explore another room of the cursed temple.

96

You mix a little water with the strange potion.

Nothing happens.

You better go back to 99 to try another combination or see whether you've missed a clue.

97

Fighting the cursed king is not going to be easy, but that's the choice you've made!

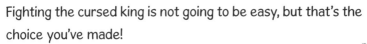

"Are you going to fight this THING? You're NUTS! I hope that you've managed to find some gear for that; otherwise, you'll get beaten to pulp!"

As you face him, the king groans and continues to stare at you with those red eyes. Without any warning, he comes at you, brandishing his sword!

You fend off his first blow, just barely. Fortunately for you, his size is also a disadvantage—you're small enough to run between his legs. In a dance of swords you never thought yourself capable of, you strike him again and again.

Not every blow hurts him—his massive armor protects him—but little by little, you chip away at his health stats. It gives you confidence.

Victory is close as you start to anticipate your opponent's every move. But, just as you are about to deliver the fatal blow, the king does something different. He picks you up and throws you. Then he charges in your direction.

It's over.

At least, that's what you think as you watch the behemoth approach. But you hadn't counted on Eeebs! He jumps on the king's face, claws out.

This is the diversion you've been waiting for! You get up and charge at full speed, sword in hand, and deliver the final blow to the cursed king!

He collapses with a final rattle and a thud, shaking the ground. . . .

You have defeated the cursed king!

Breeze! Quick! Go see how she's doing by going to 89.

98

Warning! Do not keep reading unless you've figured out how to unlock access to this area! If you haven't, go back to where you were before.

You finally arrive in the dungeon. You should be happy to be so close to your goal, but you are stunned. The room you just entered is COMPLETELY EMPTY and WHITE. There is NOTHING IN IT. Not even the shadow of a bat.

"Holy zombie chicken! What is this place?"

You look closely at the map. . . . It's the dungeon.

As you move through the room, the sound of smashing makes you turn around. The passage you just came through has disappeared. You can't return to the other rooms of the cursed temple anymore. Above you, Herobrine's face appears.

"You are more resourceful than you look, little warrior. And yet you are now imprisoned in an inescapable dungeon. HA HA HA HA HA!"

Then he disappears.

That's when you notice one of the walls looks really weird. It's a mirror! You'd heard of this type of witchcraft, but you'd never seen it before. It's captivating!

As you run your hand across the strange, cold material, an engraving catches your eye. What sorcerer could engrave something so fragile?

It's UNTHINKABLE! Here's what you read:

THE EXIT IS NEAR, BUT THE WRATH OF THE CURSED KING IS NEARER STILL! COME FORTH AND PRESENT THE POWER CUBE! LOOK AT THE LINE WHERE THE WOOD AND LAVA MEET. THE MIRROR WILL TELL YOU WHERE TO GO.

"Runt, I think you have to put the cube in front of a mirror! The solution must be a number on the sides the engraving mentions!"

You are stuck in the depths of the cursed temple. If you want to get out of here, you have to solve this puzzle. . . . Otherwise, you will never see the light of day again.

99

You approach the closed door. You can't open it, even using all your strength.

Engraved in the hard surface of the door, you notice a strange sign.

REMEMBER THE WORDS
IN THE PICTURE. . . .

"This symbol reminds me of a potion. How about you? But it's not just any potion—it looks like a volatile potion. If you have a strange potion in your inventory, you should try a combination to see whether you can make it volatile. If you don't have one, it might be better to return to 104 to explore, I think! Don't hesitate to write down this number, 99, somewhere so you can come back later."

100

You press one of the buttons on the levitating cube and hear a click. You let out a sigh of relief.

Meanwhile, you hear a noise from inside the cube that intrigues you.

It reminds you of the sound of TN—

BOOM!

You pressed the wrong button, and it caused an explosion! You lose consciousness.

Your adventure ends here. Go to 47.

101

You decide to go look at the room's pedestals and murals.

For the most part, the pedestals are in really bad shape. You guess that these previously held sculptures of heroes. Looking a little more closely, you discover a jukebox at the foot of one of them. Go make a note of it in your inventory!

The murals, on the other hand, have aged better. On most of them, you see a warrior with shining armor. When you look closer, you can see that he's wearing a crown.

As you marvel at this past glory, you come face to face with a vandalized mural. You see the image of the same warrior, in a triumphant pose, but someone scratched it all over.

Eeebs reads the writing left by the vandal out loud:

MAY THE CURSED KING NEVER SEE
THE LIGHT OF DAY AGAIN!

A loud noise, louder than ever, shakes the whole temple.

GGGGGEEEEEEEUUURRRRRRHHHH

You swear Eeebs just let out a yelp.

You don't feel terribly reassured. You can continue exploring the gallery of heroes by going to 95. Or you can go elsewhere.

102

You take Breeze in your arms and start running across the dungeon.

The cursed king is chasing you! He's groaning loudly and brandishing a huge iron sword.

You look all around you, but you can't see a way out! You're trapped. . . . A furious rumbling makes your skin crawl, and you sense the shadow of the cursed king loom over you.

You can feel his breath on your neck.

You don't even have the time to turn around before he hits you with all his might. If only you had diamond gear to fight him . . . You lose consciousness.

Your adventure ends here. Go to 47.

103

Warning! Do not keep reading unless you've figured out how to unlock access to this area! If you haven't, go back to where you were before.

You reach a tiny room. Inside, you find gunpowder. Make a note of it in your inventory.

You then carefully go back to the beginning to choose another kind of block to cross on. Go to 68.

104

Warning! Do not keep reading unless you've figured out how to unlock access to this area! If you haven't, go back to where you were before.

You find yourself in the alchemy lab. It looks kind of like you thought it would: a dim room with a mystical atmosphere, full of secrets.

What you were not expecting is the hundreds of potions of all colors and sizes that fill the shelves lining the walls. Unfortunately, you can't take any of them.

There is a strange picture covered in writing. There is also a brewing stand and a closed door. To go look at the picture, go to 80. To check out the brewing stand, go to 63. To try to open the door, go to 99. You can also continue exploring the second level.

105

Suddenly, you remember that the golems in your village sometimes gave flowers to passers-by.

And if . . .

You hold out one of your blue orchids to the warrior golem, and it stops dead in its tracks. Amazing! You can't believe that worked! The creature takes the flower and returns to stand next to the throne. With one last sound of scraping stone, it freezes.

A blue orchid for a diamond shield . . . that trade almost makes it free! And that's really cool, because you love free stuff!

You silently thank Breeze. After all, it was in her cloak that you found the orchids.

To continue exploring the old throne room, go to 65. You can also explore another room.

106

You take the jukebox from your inventory and put on some music.

A strange melody fills the dungeon. It's both sad and catchy. An extremely talented bard with great powers must have composed it, because you can tell that it's full of magic.

"Runt, look! A passage has just appeared! Let's go!"

Without thinking, you gather Breeze in your arms and run after the cat. You take a strange passageway that plunges into the darkness, but you can sense it's going up.

Around you, everything continues to shake, and you hear tremendous noises. The cursed temple is COLLAPSING!

Finally, you see the light of day.

"Eeebs! It's the exit! Hurry, before we get stuck in here!" you exclaim.

You have almost no strength left, but you still manage to escape the temple. The passageway leads you to the sandy beach where you first arrived.

The ground shakes as the cursed temple sinks into the water. You put Breeze down and push back a lock of hair that falls in her face. She is still unconscious, but at least she is safe! They can help her get better in the village.

As the temple sinks deeper into the dark water, Herobrine's angry voice sounds all around you: "You escaped this time, little warrior, but don't think this is over! We will meet again. . . ."

An unexpected strength rises in you, and you hear yourself screaming, "I'm counting on it! And I'll be ready!"

Determination flares in your eyes. With a final tremor, the cursed temple disappears under the water.

Congratulations!

You have saved Breeze, defeated the cursed king,
and managed to escape from the temple!

A1: HINTS AND SOLUTIONS

Hi, Runt!

In this part of the book, I'll help you solve the puzzles that are stumping you. Just go to the number corresponding to the section of the puzzle. I'll give you a hint first. If you still can't figure out how to solve the puzzle, I'll give you the solution!

25

Hint 1:
The panel mentions a very specific cube. This is a cube that you should have found in the secret archives and that you had to assemble yourself.

Hint 2:
It's the power cube! If you made it by following the directions, you just have to put it on the device, making sure that the ice side of the cube touches the ice square. You should see a number.

Solution:
If you've followed the instructions, you should see a number appear when you step back: **017**. The "1" is on the top of the cube.

26

Hint:
You know what certain symbols represent. You just need to insert those throughout the text.

Solution:
The translated text tells you to go to **45**.

40

Hint:
What if you tried to hide the lower half of the sword's blade?

Solution:
On the left of the sword, you can read "Go to." And if you hide the lower half of the blade, the number **33** appears! You just have to go there!

44

Hint:
The sign mentions extremes. It must refer to the numbers on the button on the far left and the button on the far right. Add up those two numbers. What do you get?

Solution:
To get the answer, you have to add the number of the button at the far left, so **05**, to the number of the one on the far right, so **03**. That's **05 + 03 = 08**. Now you know where you have to go in the book!

46

Hint:

You should look at the mural a little more closely. I'm sure you missed something. It seems to me that there's something to read.

Solution:

On the mural, you can read "Go to 09." Just follow the instructions!

60

Hint:

Don't forget that each symbol can appear only once per line, column, and square. So under the fish of the first line is a diamond. And under the diamond in the lower left must be a fish. . . .

Solution:

If you solve the grid correctly, you find a ball of slime in "a" and a fish in "b," which works out to **78**. This is where you have to go.

63

Hint:

You already know that the spider eye equals **10** and that the bone is **5**. So you just need to subtract those to figure out the number of feathers: **30 – 15**.

Solution:

When you do the right calculation, you get the number **15**. This is where you have to go.

Hint:

The text tells you that some blocks are not the right ones. "The correct block is not green," so it's not the emerald block. And, "It's not under the material that buckets are made of." This must mean that it's not the block that's under the iron block, since it's with iron that buckets are forged.

Solution:

The correct block is iron. It's the only one that you can choose if you follow the instructions. You know then that you have to go to **52**.

68

Hint:

Keep in mind that you can jump up to only two blocks at a time. You can easily rule out wood blocks, since you can't get farther than the first wood block.

Solution:

To reach the other side of the room, you have to jump on the dirt blocks. So you know that you have to go to **71** because that's the number on the first dirt block. You might also want to try getting across using the diamond blocks. You might find something useful. . . .

88

Hint:

Don't hesitate to use a pencil to draw a line along the paths you try. You can always erase the line afterward. What I can tell you is that I don't think the button on the top is the right one.

The correct solution is the blue button, which leads you to **82**.

93

To start with, you have to make sure that the mossy stone side of your power cube is touching the one in the book, so you have to put your cube down on the book and keep it that way. You can then rotate the cube until the symbols on the book align with those on the cube. You should be able to read something. . . .

If you've placed your cube stone-side down and rotated it, when the lava side is on the left, you'll be able to read "Go to **83**." This is where you have to go.

98

The engraving mentions a mirror. This is a mirror in real life. You have to find a mirror and put your power cube in front of it. If you place it correctly, a number should appear.

If you put the power cube up to a mirror and place it correctly, you will see the number **94** appear. The **9** is on the wood side and the **4** is on the lava side.

A2: COMBINATIONS

Here are all the things you can combine on your adventure! You can use this table to try out different combinations. For example, you could combine a safe with a key to open the safe. You can even combine an object with a place.

FIRST-LEVEL COMBINATIONS

	IRON DOOR	DEVICE WITH THREE BUTTONS	SMALL FRAME
SMALL IRON KEY	49	12	23

	FLINT AND STEEL	BUCKET OF WATER	BOOK
DESK	43	32	26

	FLINT AND STEEL	DIAMOND SWORD	BOOK
WALL HANGING	31	24	42

	FLINT AND STEEL	BOOK	DIAMOND SWORD
ZOMBIE	36	41	16

SECOND-LEVEL COMBINATIONS

	DIAMOND SWORD	BLUE ORCHID	DIAMOND SHIELD
WARRIOR GOLEM	64	105	79

	EEEBS	FLINT AND STEEL	TORCH
DARK ROOM	69	76	67

	GUNPOWDER	BLUE ORCHID	BUCKET OF WATER
STRANGE POTION	74	85	96

A3: INVENTORY

When you find an object, add a check mark next to it on this list. This will help you keep track of everything you've picked up.

- ⬡ SMALL IRON KEY
- ⬡ BOOK
- ⬡ FLINT AND STEEL
- ⬡ DIAMOND SWORD
- ⬡ BLUE ORCHID
- ⬡ POWER CUBE
- ⬡ TORCH
- ⬡ BUCKET OF WATER
- ⬡ GUNPOWDER
- ⬡ DIAMOND SHIELD
- ⬡ DIAMOND HELMET
- ⬡ STRANGE POTION
- ⬡ VOLATILE STRANGE POTION
- ⬡ JUKEBOX

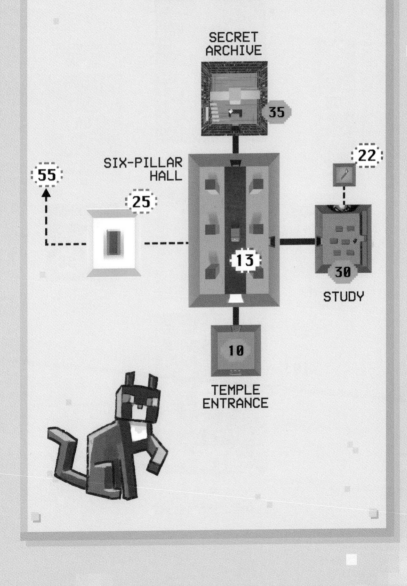

A4: MAP OF THE CURSED TEMPLE

FIRST LEVEL

SECRET
ARCHIVE

35

SIX-PILLAR
HALL

55

25

13

22

30

STUDY

10

TEMPLE
ENTRANCE

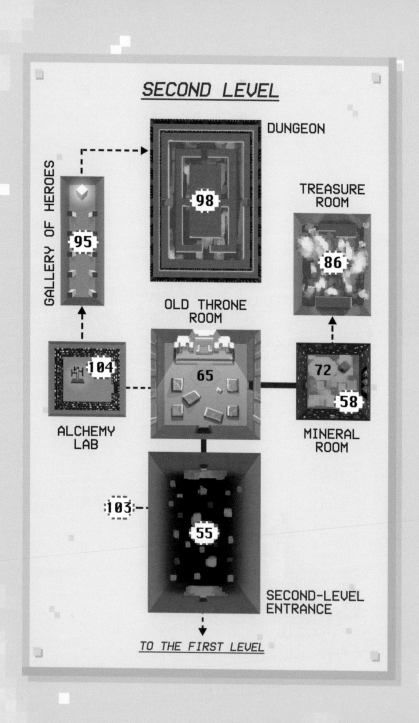

SECOND LEVEL

DUNGEON

TREASURE ROOM

GALLERY OF HEROES

OLD THRONE ROOM

ALCHEMY LAB

MINERAL ROOM

SECOND-LEVEL ENTRANCE

TO THE FIRST LEVEL

95

98

86

104

65

72

58

103

55

A5: POWER CUBE
WARNING!
DO NOT KEEP READING UNLESS THE BOOK
HAS TOLD YOU TO COME HERE!

This is the power cube. . . . It's an extremely powerful relic FULL OF MAGIC. You must craft it yourself to use it in the cursed temple.

Just follow the instructions. Don't hesitate to ask an adult for help.

If you don't want to cut your book, you can make a photocopy of the page with the cube pattern. You will need a pair of scissors and some glue.

You'll see some numbers on the cube. Don't go directly to those. It won't help!

When you're done, don't forget to go back to **45**.

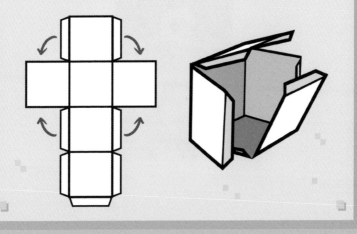